For days of light and laughter - P.B.

For Jordan - B.M.

This paperback edition first published in 2023 by Andersen Press Ltd.

First published in Great Britain in 2022 by Andersen Press Ltd.,

20 Vauxhall Bridge Road, London, SW1V 2SA, UK · Vijverlaan 48, 3062 HL Rotterdam, Nederland

Text copyright © Peter Bently 2022. Illustration copyright © Becka Moor 2022.

1 3 5 7 9 10 8 6 4 2

British Library Cataloguing in Publication Data available. ISBN 978 1 83913 060 1

X096452

The item should be returned or renewed by the last date stamped below.

Dylid dychwelyd neu adnewyddu'r eitem erbyn y dyddiad olaf sydd wedi'i stampio isod.

Newport
CITY COUNCIL
CYNGOR DINAS
Casnewydd

21-2-24.   ~~PILLGWENLLY~~

To renew visit / Adnewyddwch ar
www.newport.gov.uk/libraries

PANTEMONIUM!

Peter Bently   Becka Moor

ANDERSEN PRESS

Fred's going fishing this morning. But look!
His **pants** have got caught on the end of his **hook!**
They're his **favourite** pair, super-stretchy and **strong.**
He picks up a mouse as he drags them along!

Oh, pantemonium!

How about that?

Those underpants scoop up
the neighbour's pet cat!

Miss Yapper is taking her **dog** for a stroll —

and **into** those **undies** the pair of them **roll!**

Fred's at the baker's to buy a quick snack
and catches the cakes in his underpants sack!

BANK

BOOKS

They sweep every pastry
and bun off the shelf,

then finally sweep up the **baker** himself!

(Fred doesn't see, but he does think it's odd
that he seems to be carrying a heavier rod.)

Constable Kelly is watching it all.

She's next in those knickers —

police car and all!

BEEEP!

"Come back with our engine!"

The firefighter cries.

Oh, pantemonium!

Fred's by the zoo.

He's caught a giraffe —

and an elephant too!

"This rod's such a weight!" mutters Fred, feeling tetchy.
If only he knew that his pants were so str**etchy!**
They catch little Goldilocks quite unawares.

And soon she's got company
– in go the Bears!

Those incredible underpants stretch even

bigger when —

Oh, pantemonium!

— in goes a digger!

Next in the undies —

a great **yellow crane**!

Then, at the railway...

Fred's caught a train!

Finally Fred has arrived at the sea —
and all of the things in
his undies go free.

"How funny," thinks Fred as he stands by the shore,

"My fishing rod   feels a lot lighter once more."

But that's not the end
of this **megapants** tale.

Oh, pantemonium!

Fred's caught...

More picture books to discover from Roald Dahl Funny Prize-winning Peter Bently:

The Great Dog Bottom Swap

Skunk! Skedaddle!

The Prince and the Porker

The Great Balloon Hullaballoo

The Great Sheep Shenanigans

Find out more at www.andersenpress.co.uk